ReBoot

The Quick & the Fed
and
Medusa Bug

ReBoot

The Quick &
The Fed
and
Medusa Bug

adapted from the television
series by Russell Bell

B🍃XTREE

First published in Great Britain in 1995 by Boxtree Ltd,
Broadwall House, Broadwall, London SE1 9PL.

Copyright © Mainframe Joint Venture 1994
Licensed by Copyright Promotions Limited

10 9 8 7 6 5 4 3 2 1

ISBN: 0 7522 0600 1

A CIP catalogue entry for this book is available from
the British Library

Designed by Shoot that Tiger!

Typeset in Century by SX Composing, Rayleigh, Essex
Printed and bound in Great Britain by
Cox & Wyman Ltd, Reading, Berkshire

Introduction

'Hi, my name's Dot and I live in a cool city called Mainframe. It's a bustling, super-hi-tech metropolis. Binomes do some of the boring work, which leaves the Data Sprites like me to get on with organising things, and that can be a lot of fun.

You should see the number of problems that people bring to me at Dot's Diner, but I usually manage to solve them. Well, maybe with a bit of help from Bob, who is probably the coolest dude you will ever meet.

You see, Bob came to Mainframe from the Super Computer, which is what you might call the fast lane. Bob was a top level guardian at the Super Computer Port, kind of a cop who prevented illegal entires. But he had a major run-in with a power-hungry bad guy called Megabyte, who is a pretty nasty virus. In fact, it was while fighting to keep Megabyte out of the Super Computer that Bob was drawn into Mainframe. Now because Bob is from the Super Computer, his speed is just awesome. However, Megabyte is also pretty fast and Bob had his work cut out stopping him from taking over the whole of Mainframe.

Megabyte is always trying to take things over, but he'll have to get past Bob first, and that is far from easy. Megabyte has two heavies called Hack and Slash that help him out, but things often get pretty confused because no-one knows which one is which. Not even Hack and Slash themselves.

Megabyte isn't the only problem we have around here though. There's Hexadecimal, the Queen of Chaos and Malfunction. She lives in the City of Lost Angles which is a warped and twisted place full of nasty Nulls that she can control. All Hexadecimal wants to do is mess everything up for everybody, and we have to spend half our time making sure that she doesn't. She is very unpredictable. She has a little pet called Scuzzy who zips around being sly and devious.

Talking of pets, my little brother Enzo kind of owns a dog called Frisket. Well, he's not really Enzo's pet, he's actually pretty wild it's just that he won't let anyone except Enzo touch him, not even Bob, who Enzo worships.

When the Game Cubes come down from the sky you can see just how good Bob is. He's the best game-player in Mainframe. Also, he has a great little device called Glitch than can turn into whatever small tool or gadget he needs to get the job done. (Sometimes I wish that I had one, just to fix things around the Diner!) Now, don't get the impression that we just have fun playing games all the time. The games we play are for keeps. When a cube comes down, the sector of Mainframe it covers is transformed into the landscape of the game. If The User wins, the whole sector of Mainframe is off-lined, turned into a deep, dark hole in the city. Any sprites trapped in the sector when it goes off-line are transformed into disgusting little energy-eating slugs called nulls, and that is guaranteed to take the edge off your day.

"So, exactly what sort of things happen in Mainframe?" I can hear you ask. Turn the page and find out.'

The Quick and the Fed

The Quick and the Fed

On the edge of the computer-world known as Mainframe, there is a tower in the shape of a striking snake that threatens the grey sky with gleaming fangs. This is Silicon Tor, where Megabyte, the power-hungry computer virus, has made his sanctuary. In the centre of this tower is a massive laboratory. If you wanted to build a large, powerful device to take over the world, this would be a good place to do it. That thought had already occurred to a certain power-hungry computer virus ...

Megabyte sat in his hover-chair overseeing the final adjustments to his latest invention. It was difficult to see what it was, but most people would have worked out that

7

it spelt bad news for the citizens of Mainframe. It looked like a colossal crane with some kind of generator attached to the bottom. Massive pipes and wires ran up the crane to the very end where there was a little hand-sized, horseshoe magnet that looked far too small for the huge machine, and not very dangerous at all. That is, until you remember that the most deadly thing to computer sprites and binomes is a magnet. Even a little magnet, because it can erase them forever in no time at all. Now, this little magnet was linked to an awesome energy unit that would multiply its power a thousand times. This could account for the look of triumph that had spread across Megabyte's face. While his slug-like pet, Nibbles, tried to bite the 'busy' binomes that passed by, Megabyte sat pushing buttons on his control panel, and guards with stun sticks stood at attention nearby.

Finally, everything seemed to be ready. Megabyte grinned horribly and pushed a button on his control panel. A low humming

8

started to built to a deafening whine and the arm of the crane began to extend upwards, like a telescope. Up and up it went, towards a huge round hole in the roof of the Tor. Sparks of energy flew from the arm as the power surged along it and gathered in the magnet at the end. Suddenly a shaft of power shot from the magnet into the calm grey heavens, which became stormy and began to swirl like a whirlpool, opening a hole in the very sky itself.

'It's opening, Nibbles,' declared Megabyte in a triumphant voice, 'my path to the Super Computer!' He squeezed Nibbles with excitement, almost squashing him completely. The electro-magnet continued to pour energy upwards as the sky boiled, and dark clouds swirled in the vortex. Megabyte stared upwards with flashes of energy reflecting in his eyes.

'More worlds,' he declared, 'more servants, more power.'

Suddenly, something flashed into the room in a blur of speed. It was Megabyte's old rival Bob, riding on a zip-board. He stopped just long enough to add 'Not!' to Megabyte's speech. Then he shot off again before Megabyte could work out what was happening. Megabyte managed to utter a puzzled 'What?' and dropped Nibbles in a squidgy heap as Bob skimmed along the arm of the crane, hovering inches above the pipes and rigging.

Several of the smarter binomes realised what was happening and gave chase on zip-boards of their own, shouting, 'Get him! It's Bob! Stop him!'

Strangely, Megabyte didn't look too concerned. In fact, he grinned, watching Bob with interest. 'He'll erase if he gets within ten bits of that magnet,' he said, quite cheered up by the prospect.

However, Bob wasn't that stupid. Reaching the top of the arm, Bob hovered on his zip-board. Then he raised his left hand. There, on his wrist was Glitch, an all purpose device that could transform into any tool he needed.

'Glitch,' he ordered, 'Cutters.' Glitch knew what he wanted, and transformed into a whirling star with razor sharp blades that Bob sent flying at the end of the crane, cutting loose vital wires and causing the entire telescopic arm of the crane to topple sideways until it leant against the side of the hole in the ceiling.

Various sections fell to the floor of the laboratory where binomes scattered shouting, 'Augh! Look out! Backspace! Backspace!'

Megabyte could see he was going to have to get involved. He thumped his control panel angrily and a platform rose up through the laboratory floor. There, standing on the platform, were the legs he used when he wasn't in his hover chair. He hovered across the lab and lowered himself into place on the legs.

Meanwhile Bob was looking at the still-smouldering magnet at the top of the crane. He knew he couldn't afford to touch it, so, raising his wrist, he gave a command: 'Glitch, auto-stow.'

Glitch changed into a pair of tongs on a telescopic arm. The tongs reached out, grasped the magnet and stowed it safely in a lead box fitted to Bob's waist. However, as soon as he had done this, he heard a bellow of rage and looked down the arm of the crane to see Megabyte climbing towards him in animal-like bounds. He didn't look very happy.

He reached the top in no time and launched himself at Bob, but Bob was far too fast. He shot out of the way on his zip-board. Megabyte grabbed at thin air and plunged over the side of the building, just managing to shoot out a claw and grab the outside wall where he clung, fuming, as Bob flew past, waving pleasantly.

'Later!' shouted Bob cheerily and shot off on his zip-board with a whoosh. Megabyte's eyes narrowed in anger as he thought about all the horrible things he would do to Bob when he finally caught him. Then he began the hard climb back into his lab where he could take out his frustrations on a few of the slower-moving binomes. Bob headed for Dot's Diner. He felt he deserved a little refreshment.

The assorted binomes in the Diner swivelled their different shaped heads as Bob strolled in, carrying his zip-board. After all, Bob *was* a bit of a hero in Mainframe. Suddenly, out of nowhere, something rushed at Bob and launched itself at him. He just had time to turn his head before it hit him, knocking him over and pinning him to the ground, but it was only Enzo, Dot's little brother and Bob's number one fan. The youngster couldn't talk fast enough. 'Major coolness out there, Bob! I heard you royally kicked Megabyte's bit map. Think there'll be a game soon? Think I could go into the game with you, huh? I could be your co-pilot or your deputy or . . .'

Dot called his name: 'Enzo!'

'Yeah, Dot?' he replied.

'It's not good for business when you sit on the customers,' she pointed out.

'Oh, sorry. Here Bob,' said Enzo, helping Bob to his feet.

As Bob stood up, Cecil the maitre d' came whizzing over on his mounted brass ceiling rail. He was like a TV with a picture of a French waiter on the screen. He had a moustache and a bow-tie and two mechanical arms that stuck out from the sides of his box-like body. He tended to wave these arms around a lot when he talked.

'Table for two?' he inquired in his professional waiter voice.

'Yeah, Seesull, please,' replied Bob. Cecil did *not* like the way Bob pronounced his name.

'That's *Cecil*!' he said and looked around the Diner. There were plenty of seats free but Cecil shooed them across the room with his dangly mechanical arms.

'Wait at the bar, wait at the bar,' he said like a school teacher to a pair of naughty children. Bob and Enzo headed for the bar as all the sprites and binomes in the Diner greeted Bob.

'Hey, Bob . . . How's it running . . . Good to see ya, Bob . . . Attaboy, Bob.'

14

Dot was already sitting at the bar.

'Care to join me, Bob?' she asked. Bob smiled a little shyly.

'Uh, sure, thanks, Dot,' he said as Enzo jumped on to a seat. Bob lowered himself on to a stool. Unfortunately it wasn't there and he landed on the floor with a thump. Dot covered her mouth with her hand and tried not to laugh, which was far from easy. Bob leapt up, scowling.

'Somebody stole my stool!' he declared, but no-one was rude enough to point out that there hadn't been one there in the first place.

'Cecil,' said Dot, trying to change the subject. 'A drink for Bob.'

Cecil appeared behind them.

'Of course, ma'am,' he said politely, then at the top of his voice he bellowed: 'Tall cool one, on track one!'

At the far end of the counter a set of little traffic lights went quickly from red to yellow to green. A flap opened and a tall shake with a lid and a straw on top shot out of the little door. (You could tell it was cool, because it was wearing sunglasses.) It whizzed once round the oval counter like a racing car, much too fast for anyone to grab it. Then it jumped on to the floor and raced out of the Diner, leaving the doors flapping behind it. Dot looking at Bob with a satisfied smile.

'Dot's Diner,' she said proudly. 'The fastest food in Mainframe.'

Bob licked his dry lips. 'This is true,' he sighed. When you live inside a computer, fast-moving milk-shakes wearing sunglasses seem almost normal.

Suddenly Enzo noticed the lead box fixed to Bob's belt. 'Awww, cool. What's this?' he asked. Bob placed the box on the counter with a thud.

'It's a magnet,' he said casually.

Everyone in the Diner leapt out of their seats in a panic and scrambled round, looking for somewhere to hide.

'Magnet!' they screamed. 'Run for your code! Look out! Aueegh!!'

Bob sat quietly until the panic had died down.

'It's okay,' he said, tapping the lead box, 'it's shielded.'

Enzo and Dot peeped out cautiously from their hiding places. They smiled nervously. The various customers returned to their seats, looking a bit embarrassed.

'Oh, it's shielded. Thank goodness. You scared us there, Bob.' They should have known that Bob would never put them in any danger.

Dot looked at the lead box with concern. 'You'd better get that to old man Pearson's data dump down in sector one zero zero one,' she said.

'I will,' replied Bob. 'Thanks.' It was then that Bob noticed Enzo staring at his left wrist, where Glitch was attached. Bob decided to give Enzo a treat.

'Go ahead,' Enzo,' he said, 'give Glitch a try.'

Enzo's face lit up with excitement. 'Really?' he said, beaming. 'Alphanumeric!' he exclaimed, which was probably the greatest compliment he could pay to anything.

Bob handed Glitch to Enzo who held it up, thinking hard. 'Glitch . . .' he commanded, 'uh . . . hammer.' There was a *click-whirr-click* and Glitch changed into a hammer. Enzo was delighted. 'Flashlight,' he said, and with a *click-click-snap* Glitch converted into a flashlight. The beam shot across the Diner, almost dazzling Bob, who smiled, glad to see his little friend having so much fun.

Enzo was really getting the hang of it now and decided to try for something a little more adventurous. 'Jackhammer!' he said confidently. There was a *zzz-click-click* and Enzo suddenly found himself riding on top of a fully functioning road drill that was totally out of control.

'Oh-whagh-oagh-oagh-oagh-oagh!' went Enzo. In fact, the whole Diner was shaking and customers were being jolted out of their chairs. More worrying was the fact that the little lead box had vibrated itself to the edge of the counter. Bob, despite being vibrated across the floor by the jackhammer, acted as swiftly as he could in the circumstances.

'Glitch! Stop!' he commanded. There was a *click-click-hiss-click* and Glitch returned to its usual shape and shot across the room to dock with the unit on Bob's left wrist. Enzo hovered briefly in mid air, wearing a surprised expression, then he fell to the floor with a thud. The lead box came to a stop right at the edge of the counter, where it rocked back and forth. Dot, who was standing right in front of the box, looked on, horrified.

The box finally teetered too far and fell to the floor where it sprang open. The small black magnet inside buzzed like an angry bee and flew through the air towards Dot. There was nothing she could do. The magnet hit her in the centre of her forehead and stuck there. Dot sparked with static and began to fade, becoming more and more transparent with every moment. Enzo shouted, 'Sis!!' not knowing what to do.

Bob jumped forward, and snapped a command to his wrist unit: 'Glitch, auto-stow.'

Glitch immediately transformed into the

telescopic tongs, shooting out to grab the magnet and stow it back in the lead box. As soon as the magnet was removed, Dot fell to the floor in a faint, still looking dangerously transparent. Bob rushed forward and scooped her up, carrying her over to a booth and laying her down gently while Enzo looked on with concern.

'What have I done?' he cried. 'Poor Dot. Erased by her own brother in the prime of her input/output. She's too young to end file, too young to quit without saving. It's all my fault. If only I'd – '

Bob had put his hand over Enzo's mouth.

'We'll get her help, Enzo. Don't panic!' Bob looked desperately around the room wondering what to do. He decided to panic.

'Doesn't anyone here know how to reverse a magnet erasure?' he shouted. All the customers shook their heads sadly. Cecil, however, held up a finger.

'No, but Phong would, sir . . .' Cecil was about to carry on but Bob had disappeared. There was just the sound of the front doors swinging back and forth. When Bob had something important to do he didn't hang about.

GO TO

The Principle Office is a large, central, circular building that towers over Mainframe like a massive, metal football. It's the heart of this land and is connected to the rest of Mainframe by five thin bridges. This is the home of Phong, a very old and wise sprite who has seen pretty much everything in his time and is always a good person to go to for advice. There's only one drawback. You have to play computer Ping-Pong with him. Then, if you win, he will help you out. Most people don't win.

This time Bob was playing him, and getting frustrated at the waste of precious time. The computer-generated walls of the game court surrounded them, and the game puck hovered in mid air. Force fields glowed around their hands and feet, allowing them to glide back and forth and to strike the puck without damaging themselves.

'Uh, Phong, Dot needs help *now*? As in not later?' But Phong was focused on the game.

'Shhh. Concentration is important,' he said, knocking the puck back and forth between his hands. Suddenly, Phong struck the puck and it went flying across the court. Bob didn't have time for a polite game today though, and he returned the puck with an almighty smash. It sped back across the court and hit Phong on the side of his head, making it spin round.

'Ah, you have good backspin, my son,' he said when his head had stopped spinning, and a little binome popped out of the puck to agree.

'You're telling me,' it said, looking dazed.

'Now that you have whomped me at my favourite game,' said Phong, 'you have proven yourself worthy of my vast knowledge and endless wisdom.' Then he looked confused.

'What was the question?'

22

Bob's frustration grew. Phong was certainly wise, but he was very old and sometimes did things a little too slowly for a high-speed sprite like Bob.

'I told you,' Bob said patiently, 'it's Dot. She's been partially erased by a magnet and they said you would know how to return her to normal.'

Phong put his hand to his chin.

'Hmmm . . .' he muttered to himself. 'Magnetic erasure, eh? The source code accelerates an unstable file fragmentation leading to a complete delete.'

'Whoa,' said Bob, 'you lost me, Phong. Can you repeat that?'

Phong looked confused again.

'Probably not. But I can tell you that Dot needs to access some really, really, REALLY slow food. It will decelerate her accelerated condition and return her to normal.' Phong suddenly began to push Bob towards the door with arms that telescoped out from his body.

'Well,' he shouted, 'what are you waiting

for? Any shock or sudden movement could completely destabilise her. Hurry! You don't have all second you know.' (This might sound like a strange thing to say, but inside a computer a second is a very long time indeed.)

Bob headed back to the Diner as fast as he could.

GO TO

A crowd of concerned citizens gathered round as Bob explained to Enzo and Dot what Phong had told him. He was checking an address on a pocket vid-window.

'. . . and he knew a place that serves this kind of slow food.' He read from the screen: 'Al's Wait 'n' Eat...' Then he looked up, with a worried expression. '. . . Level Thirty One.'

Enzo was shocked. 'Level Thirty One? No way.'

Dot was very weak, but she still struggled to sit up and tried to speak.

'Level-Al? You-dangerous-can't-down-go-Thirty-there.'

Bob put his finger to her lips. 'Shh,' he said. 'Not to worry. I've got this all figured out.'

But Dot was still trying to tell him something. 'But-business, my-Bob-problem-too-Al's-far-vid-window . . .'

Unfortunately she wasn't making much sense. Bob interrupted her.

'Not another word,' he announced. 'You do the relaxing, I'll do the saving, okay?' Then he looked at the others in the Diner. 'Man,' he said quietly, 'she's really out of it.'

Enzo began jumping around at Bob's feet like an excited little animal.

'Ooooh, oooh! Can I go with you? Level Thirty One? Can I, can I, huh?' Bob looked at Enzo with a serious expression. He knew he couldn't take the boy to Level Thirty One, it was much too dangerous, but he didn't want to upset him.

'I'm counting on you here,' said Bob, 'and so is your sister.'

Enzo stopped bouncing. 'She is?' he asked, suddenly aware of his responsibility.

'Yes,' said Bob seriously. 'Make sure she accesses plenty of down time and doesn't touch anything that's not grounded.'

Enzo snapped to attention and saluted solemnly.

'Aye aye, Bob. You can count on me,' he declared and Bob knew that he meant it. Satisfied that he could do no more at the Diner, Bob jumped on to his zip-board. The sooner he came back with some slow food, the better were Dot's chances of survival.

The customers cleared a path as he shouted, 'Hang in there Dot! Bob's on the job.' Then he shot out of the Diner with a whoosh and headed for the lower levels.

Dot tried to sit up. 'No-far-too-but-window,' she mumbled, but even if Bob had been there he wouldn't have known what she was talking about. Enzo gently pushed her back down.

'Dot,' he whispered kindly, 'you heard Bob. Now shush.'

GO TO

Imagine streets full of rubbish. Dark shadows flitting between the trash cans. Neon lights flicker and spark among the twisted pipes and scaffolding. A pair of nulls fight viciously in the dark. That's Level Thirty One on a good day.

Bob zipped along the shadowy streets and came to rest outside a particularly nasty looking building with a sign that said AL's WAIT 'N' EAT. Bob thought it looked like one of the roughest places he had ever seen.

He opened the door and stepped in. He had been wrong. It *was* the roughest place he had ever seen. As he stepped through the door a variety of heads swivelled round to see who had arrived, and to see if he would be worth erasing for fun or profit or, ideally, both. The only sounds in the room were low, angry growls as Bob headed through the scowling crowd.

'Whoa,' he muttered to himself. 'Tough

room.' He decided to finish his business there and get out as soon as possible.

He approached the bar. Al's waiter was asleep with his head on the counter. Bob slapped the counter with his hand. 'Hello!' he shouted.

The waiter lifted his head very slowly and looked Bob in the eye. Then he spoke in the slowest voice Bob had ever heard.

'May I take your order?' he yawned. Bob realised that he'd have to hurry things up a bit.

'This is an emergency!' he announced. 'I need slow food to go ... FAST!'

The waiter turned to the serving hatch behind him, laughing very slowly.

'That's a good one,' he drawled. 'Did you hear that, Al?'

A voice from somewhere deep in the building came back. 'What?' said Al, sounding like he had just woken up. The waiter turned back to Bob to explain the situation.

'Slow food doesn't go fast. That's why it's slow.' He pointed to a box in front of him.

'There's a counter on the counter. If you want to order some food, take a number.' Then he drifted off to do something slow elsewhere.

Bob picked a number from the counter and looked at it. 'Four thousand and ninety six ... Must be the lunch crowd,' he said hopefully.

The waited drifted back with a plate of food. 'Now serving number three,' he announced.

Bob's face fell. If he was going to save Dot, he couldn't afford to wait that long.

GO TO

Megabyte's tower rang with the sound of welding and hammering as viral binomes struggled to repair the damage that Bob had caused, but Megabyte knew the repairs would be useless without the magnet. He summoned his two lieutenants, Hack and Slash. Megabyte was never quite sure which was Hack and which was Slash. Unfortunately, Hack and Slash didn't seem to be too sure who was who either, which led to a certain amount of confusion.

'I have a function for you, Hack and Slash!' boomed Megabyte, looking at them in turn, as if trying to work out which was which.

'I'm ... Hack ... He's Slash,' said the two binomes, sharing the sentence between them. Then they began to argue about who was who.

Megabyte's eyes narrowed in anger. 'Let's not waste memory on unimportant details,' he growled. 'I need that magnet. I want you to search and retrieve Bob.'

Hack and Slash beeped and clicked, saying, 'Bob ... Magnet ... No ... Problem.' Then they spun around and shot off towards Level Thirty One.

Meanwhile, back at the slow food restaurant, Bob was sitting in a booth looking miserable. He didn't know what he could do to get served any faster. In a nearby seat sat a large, aggressive looking Number Seven. A small serving binome walked by and the Seven burped at it fiercely, making it jump. The frightened binome scurried off.

Bob turned to a binome sitting at his booth and asked him, 'What's the deal with Seven? Why's everybody afraid of him?'

The binome answered, 'Because seven ate nine,' and laughed. This was apparently a really good joke on Level Thirty One.

Bob couldn't stand the frustration any more. He crossed the room and banged on the counter again, shouting at the waiter, 'Can't you process my food any faster?'

The waiter looked up very slowly and replied in his slow drawl, 'Look, pal, I gotta feed this whole room, I got a partner on my back for this big take-out order, and Al back there only runs at three decahertz.'

A confused voice came from the back room. 'What!?' shouted Al, which was pretty much all he ever said.

The waiter continued explaining the situation to Bob. 'You gotta wait on-line like everyone else! Okay?'

The waiter handed a container of slow food to a big, fat, bad-tempered-looking Number Eight. Bob saw his chance and jumped in front of the porky binome.

'Help me please! I need your food on a matter of life and death.'

'Zip off, punk,' replied the Number Eight, 'I've been waiting for this since I was Four.'

Bob realized he wasn't going to get anywhere arguing with that particular number. He wondered what he could do next. Then he decided that hiding would be a good idea, because there was a mighty crash, and the door was smashed off its hinges as Hack and Slash arrived. All the binomes in the room looked frightened as the two heavies rolled towards the counter. The very same counter that Bob had chosen to hide behind, in fact. The waiter looked particularly worried about the presence of his new customers.

'W-What are you doing here?' he stuttered. 'We already paid Megabyte. Don't smash the place up again.' But Hack and Slash weren't taking any notice, they were looking around, trying to find Bob.

Suddenly, a large vid-window of Megabyte appeared in the middle of the restaurant.

'Everyone,' he boomed, with all the charm of a hungry crocodile, 'I'm looking for a dear friend. Have you seen him lately?' A picture of Bob appeared on the screen. This gave Bob an idea. Everyone in the restaurant was clearly afraid of upsetting Megabyte, especially with Hack and Slash there, so maybe he could do a deal. Bob reached over from his hiding place behind the counter and tugged at the waiter.

'Care to trade?' he whispered. The waiter looked down at him with a frightened expression.

'What?' he hissed. He was willing to listen to any ideas at the moment.

'You give me food ... I'll get rid of your friends.'

This sounded like a very good idea to the waiter.

'Sure! You got a deal.' He handed Bob a carton of slow food, hoping that Bob could deliver his side of the bargain. He needn't have worried. Bob stowed the food container on his belt, grabbed his zip-board and leapt on to the counter.

'Here I am, Megabyte,' he declared to the vid-window. Hack and Slash instantly swivelled to face him. 'I'll come without trouble,' he said, 'but on one condition.'

'What's . . . That?' said Hack and Slash between them.

'You have to catch me first,' announced Bob, and with that he jumped on to his zip-board and flew, full speed, at Megabyte's vid-window. He went straight through it, erasing it, and shot out of the door like a rocket.

Hack and Slash shouted, 'Hey . . . Stop!!' and rushed after him.

Outside they had two massive armoured hover-transports – ABC's: Armoured Binome Carriers. They were in such a hurry to give chase that they didn't even waste time getting in. They just jumped onto the crash grills on the front of their vehicles and ordered the drivers to give chase, shouting confused orders that were really no help to anyone. They knew that if Bob escaped they would be in big trouble with Megabyte, and they certainly didn't want that.

Bob zipped through the narrow streets with the speed and skill he had gained from his time in the Super Computer. He was the fastest sprite on a zip-board in the whole of Mainframe, but he knew that the high powered ABC's chasing him were faster. He took a sudden left on to a winding ramp that led to the higher levels, going at an incredible speed. He thought he must have lost his pursuers but they came crashing round the corner, knocking down trees and shouting encouragement to their terrified drivers. They were gaining on Bob now and they both reached out for him with their free hands, hoping to snatch him off the zip-board.

Suddenly the game alarm blared and a booming voice filled the air: 'WARNING: INCOMING GAME. WARNING: INCOMING GAME.'

Bob looked up and saw the familiar storm in the sky that meant a game cube was coming down. And when he saw the cube descending he realized that it was going to land right in front of him. He made a decision and decided to go for it. His zip-board skimmed the ground at top speed as he headed for the stretch of road where the game cube would land. Bob realized that he couldn't outrun his pursuers, he would have to out-think them. Fortunately this wasn't too difficult. He quickly tapped out a command on Glitch and a massive vid-window of Bob's face appeared in front of Hack and Slash, who screeched to a halt as the giant face spoke.

'You're never going to catch me before the game docks and the wall closes,' said Bob from the huge screen.

'Why ... Not?' asked Hack and Slash, looking puzzled.

Bob smiled, taking his time with the answer. 'Because you stopped,' he grinned, and the vid-window vanished, leaving them with a view of Bob shooting away from them on his zip-board. Hack and Slash looked at each other in horror.

'Logic ... Error ... Logic ... Error,' they intoned, realizing they had been tricked. If they had had feet they would have kicked themselves. They shot off after Bob, determined not to be deceived again. This time they were sure they would catch him. Bob looked over his shoulder. He had managed to get a lead on them. He hoped it would be enough.

Hack and Slash knew that if Bob managed to make it into the game they would lose him. They had to go for it as well. Bob had timed his run perfectly. He ducked and shot under the game cube just before it docked. But Hack and Slash were right behind him.

'We're ... Going ... To ... Make ... It. We're ... Going ... To ... Make ... It!' they shouted.

Back in his tower, Megabyte watched his two henchmen on a vid-window. 'They're *not* going to make it,' he muttered to himself.

He was right. The massive game cube docked in the middle of the road. Nothing in Mainframe can penetrate a game cube and Hack and Slash were no exception. Their ABC's smashed into the cube and the chase was over.

Back in his tower, Megabyte sighed and pushed his comms button.

'Clean-up crew, Level One,' he ordered. He hated to be beaten.

The problems for Bob, however, were only just beginning, because now he was in the game.

As soon as the cube had docked it had transformed that area of Mainframe into a medieval landscape. Bob looked around at the rolling hills, the little country cottages and the huge, white castle on the hill. There were blue skies and distant mountains, and everything looked very peaceful. Unfortunately, in a game, things never stayed peaceful for very long.

'I know this game,' said Bob. 'It looks like Castles and . . .'

Before he could finish, a large white knight in armour rushed past him and knocked him flying with a powerful blow.

'. . . Knights,' finished Bob from where he lay on the ground, shaken by the sudden attack.

A booming voice echoed around the hills: 'GAME COMMENCE!' and Bob watched as the white knight ran off towards the distant castle.

Suddenly Bob heard a distant girl's voice. 'Help,' it cried. 'Please help me!'

He jumped to his feet when he recognized the voice. 'Dot!' he said to himself, then he shouted, 'Hang on, I'm coming!' in his best heroic voice.

Bob touched the icon on his chest and gave the game command, 'REBOOT!' A gleaming suit of golden armour appeared around him. Now he was ready to take part in the game. Unfortunately the White Knight had a good head start. He had to think fast.

She needed this food. If the White Knight

grabbed Dot in her condition she could *really* be in distress. He had to get to the castle first. He frantically tried to remember the details of the game he was in. Then suddenly it came to him. He needed some seriously fast transport.

He rushed over to the nearby barn and went inside. A moment later, the doors crashed open and he swooped out across the landscape, riding on the back of a magnificent blue dragon. It was the only way to travel. He urged the dragon to gain height and headed off towards the castle to rescue Dot. Things were looking up.

But not for long. Suddenly, from nowhere, the White Knight leapt on to the dragon behind Bob and tried to throw him off. But Bob was too fast, and with one mighty swipe he knocked the White Knight from the dragon's back.

'Hey, access your own dragon!' he cried, as his opponent tumbled towards the ground.

Unfortunately for Bob, this was exactly what he did. Another dragon swooped out of the sky and caught the White Knight neatly on its back. The chase was on.

Bob wheeled his dragon round and dived into a narrow valley, trying to lose his opponent in the rocky canyon. But still the knight was right behind him, and to make matters worse, his rival's dragon began spitting balls of fire that shot past Bob's head like flaming cannon-balls. It would only be a matter of time before one hit him.

Bob kicked the sides of his dragon and tried to do a complex manoeuvre to escape the deadly fire-balls, but his dragon just made an awful clunking sound and started to fly all over the place.

'Hey!' shouted Bob, looking down at his dragon. 'Who's in there anyway?'

A squeaky hatch opened on the dragon's back and Bob could see the waiter from Al's Wait 'n' Eat restaurant sitting inside dragon, struggling with the controls. It was clear that he was not a very experienced pilot. He looked up at Bob.

'It's just me,' he said, frantically pulling

on two levers, 'and Al's working on the fire-breathing part.'

A familiar 'What?' echoed from the depths of the dragon.

'Oh great!' said Bob. Of all the citizens of Mainframe, he had to end up with those two. Still, he had to make the best of it. He shouted into the open hatch, 'Get with the program! If we don't stop that White Knight, we're all history.'

And he was right, for if a sprite is defeated in a game he becomes a Null, a disgusting little energy-eating slug, forced to scavenge for any source of power in the very lowest levels of Mainframe.

The waiter knew this well.

'Okay, here goes,' he said, pulling on the control levers. The dragon shot forward, almost causing Bob to fall off, but at least it looked like the waiter was getting the hang of things. This was good news, because the White Knight was swooping towards them with a long lance and a shield, looking like he meant business.

Bob accessed his own lance and shield and weighed the unfamiliar weapon in his hands. By now the White Knight was on a collision course, and looking very comfortable with his own lance. Bob lowered the visor of his helmet with a metallic creak. Then he spurred his dragon into the attack. It coughed and clunked a bit, then it shot backwards, jerked sideways, and finally soared forwards, much to Bob's relief. The two dragons were now flying directly towards each other at a fantastic speed. Bob steadied the lance and grasped his shield firmly.

'That's it,' he called through the open hatch. 'Steady!' The waiter was too busy pulling and yanking at the levers to reply.

At the last minute the White Knight rolled his dragon sideways. Bob responded immediately, rolling his dragon the other way so that they passed head to head. There was a deafening clang. Bob's lance broke in two, but his aim had been good. The White Knight was thrown from his mount by the tremendous impact of Bob's lance. For a moment it looked as if Bob had won, but the White Knight's dragon swooped down and scooped him out of mid-air again. The battle wasn't over yet.

Bob was still stunned from the impact and he'd lost the broken lance and his helmet. His dragon was hovering motionless as the White Knight soared towards them. The waiter popped his head out of the hatch.

'I think Al's getting the hang of the furnace,' he said proudly. Bob glanced upwards and saw his opponent diving in for the kill.

'Uh, gentlemen? Major problems at six o'clock.'

'What?' cried Al from inside the dragon.

The White Knight was almost upon them when Bob's dragon began to rumble and vibrate in a very worrying fashion. Then, just before the White Knight struck, there was a deafening belching sound and a huge sheet of fire shot from the mouth of Bob's dragon, engulfing his opponent. The White Knight's dragon flashed and sparked with

◆ Dot zip-boarded back to the Diner.

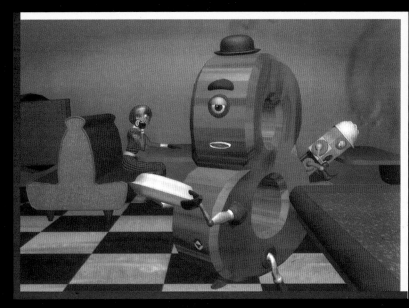

◆ 'Zip off punk', said Number Eight.
'I've been waiting for this since I was four.'

◆ With a burst of energy, Bob threw the skeleton back and stood waiting for the next phase of attack in the Castles and Knights game.

◆ 'It's mega embarrassing,' moaned Enzo.
'I wanted to reboot as a knight like you . . . not a damsel in this dress!'

◆ Just the day for a picnic.

◆ Hexadecimal erupted out of the ground
wearing an extremely angry mask.

◆ 'Really, Hexadecimal,' sighed Megabyte.
'I really don't have time for this.'

◆ The energy sped onwards like a wave of change,
returning the whole of Mainframe to normal.

static. They had scored a direct hit and the White Knight lost control of his mount. Bob smiled and patted his dragon.

'Nice belching!' he shouted into the hatch, but he knew the battle was far from over and he was running short of time. He looked towards the castle on the hill and made a decision. Leaning over the hatch, he shouted down to the waiter. 'How about keeping the White Knight busy while I access the damsel?' he asked.

The waiter gave him the thumbs up sign. 'You got it, Bob,' he declared and, after a quick battle with the control levers, the dragon flew off towards the castle. However, the waiter still hadn't quite mastered the controls and they were heading straight for a large, round stained glass window in the side of the castle's main tower.

Bob had to think fast. Fortunately he was very good at thinking fast. He stood up on the back of the dragon and, pointing his left arm at the window, he summoned Glitch.

Glitch flew from his wrist and attached

itself to the stained glass window. Immediately the window exploded into thousands of coloured fragments that began to spin round and round like a whirlpool. A hole appeared in the centre of the whirlpool and grew rapidly while the crystal fragments spun around the outside. At the last moment, Bob leapt from the dragon, diving straight through the hole. The waiter yanked on the controls and the dragon swooped sideways, narrowly missing the tower. Then it soared off, back towards the hills where the White Knight was preparing his next attack.

Bob flew through the window and hit the floor rolling. Behind him, the separate fragments of the window began to join together again, like an explosion in reverse. Bob rolled to his feet and raised his arm. Glitch flew across the room and docked on his wrist. He often wondered what he'd do without it.

He looked around the great hall. It was a long room lined with stone pillars, dimly lit with flickering torches that were mounted on the walls. A faint cry echoed through the corridors of the castle.

'Help! . . . Help!'

'I'm coming, Dot!' he called and headed across the hall.

The cry seemed to be coming from an open door at the far end of the great room. He headed for the door. In the centre of the hall was a stone altar, and lying on top of the altar was a skeleton with a sword sticking out of its ribs. Bob didn't like the look of the skeleton much but he thought the sword might come in handy.

'Don't bother to get up. I'm just passing through,' he said cheerily, as he pulled the sword free and headed for the door.

He was halfway there when he heard a low growl and a dry rattling noise behind him that sounded suspiciously like bones rubbing against stone. He decided not to look round and rushed towards the open door, but a heavy, spiked grill slid down in front of it, sealing the room.

He turned round and saw the skeleton rising from the stone slab. It had accessed another sword that it was now gripping in its bony hand. It didn't look very friendly, especially when it rushed at him and swung the sword at his head. He manged to block the blow with his own sword but the skeleton just kept coming, raining blows at him with incredible force. They battled on around the hall, the clangs of their swords echoing off the stone walls. Bob swung his sword as hard as he could but the skeleton blocked it and they stood there, swords locked together in a trial of strength.

Bob looked into the skeleton's face and said through gritted teeth, 'You really should . . . lie down . . . You look . . . terrible.'

With a burst of energy Bob threw the skeleton back and stood, waiting for the next attack, glad of the brief rest.

But the skeleton didn't attack. Instead, it raised its hand and made a 'Come here' gesture with its fingers. Bob thought this odd but suddenly the floor beneath his feet began to move towards the skeleton, exposing a deep pit behind him. At the bottom of the pit were rows of sharp spikes.

Bob was right on the edge of the pit when the skeleton attacked again. The force of the first blow knocked his shield across the room, and the second sent his sword spinning off in the other direction. The skeleton prepared to finish him off but Bob made a quick decision and jumped backwards into the deadly pit behind him. The skeleton advanced to look into the pit, expecting to see Bob in a heap at the bottom. He was in for a surprise. Bob had grabbed the edge of the pit with his right hand and, pointing his left hand, he shot Glitch upwards, into the ribcage of the skeleton and shouted a desperate command, 'Glitch! Vid-window! Large icons!'

The skeleton looked down at the tiny device hovering in its chest, clearly unimpressed, but suddenly Glitch transformed into a massive vid-window with huge red and yellow letters saying 'WHAAM!' The skeleton was blown apart as the vid-window expanded, and Bob clambered over the side of the pit as the bones showered down on to the stone floor around him with a dry clatter.

'Good work, Glitch!' he exclaimed as the device returned to its docking port on his wrist. The grill covering the doorway at the far end of the hall disappeared with a grating sound.

'Help!' The cry rang out again, but this time it sounded nearer. Bob grabbed the skeleton's sword and ran through the door. He bounded up the stairs of the tower and leapt into the room at the top, ready for anything.

Well, almost anything. There in front of him was Enzo, dressed like a medieval lady in a long pink dress and a tall pointed hat with a veil hanging from the point. He was holding an electronic megaphone.

'Bob!' he shouted.

Bob was stunned. 'Enzo?' he said incredulously. He was *sure* he had heard Dot. The reason for this soon became obvious when Enzo raised the megaphone and spoke through it.

'Am I glad to see you,' said Enzo, in an electronically altered voice that sounded just like Dot. The he lowered the megaphone and pleaded with Bob. 'You've gotta help me delete these stupid clothes! It's mega-embarrassing. I wanted to reboot as a knight like you . . . not a damsel in this dress.'

Bob gave his little friend a look-over. 'That colour is you,' he declared, smiling. Then he remembered the kid's usual habit. 'Hey. Why haven't you bowled me over yet?'

Enzo looked terribly ashamed as he pulled the front of the stiff dress aside, revealing his legs which dangled helplessly in mid air. He wasn't tall enough to reach the floor. Bob couldn't help grinning, but then he suddenly recalled why he was there.

'Where's Dot? I'm supposed to be saving her, remember?'

As he said this, there was a whooshing noise outside the window and The White

Knight and Dot tumbled from the back of a dragon on whose back they had been fighting and landed in the room with a loud clatter of armour and weapons.

'She's right there, Bob,' said Enzo helpfully.

Bob stood open mouthed, staring at the struggling heap on the floor. To his amazement, Dot was no longer partially erased. In fact, she was looking pretty strong as she battled with the White Knight.

'Dot?' shouted Bob, happily. 'You're ... you're better.'

Dot dived sideways to avoid a crushing blow from a spiked club that shattered the wooden bannister behind her.

'Not for long!' she replied, out of breath. 'I can't fight him forever ...' She ducked and another blow whistled over her head. 'At least, not by myself.'

Bob suddenly realized that he wasn't being much help.

'Oh, right, I'm coming,' he declared, and joined Dot in the swordplay, attacking with all his might.

The White Knight swung the deadly spiked club at Dot. Bob parried it with lightning speed but his sword was smashed in two by the impact. He stood looking at the little stump of sword in his hand with a rather disappointed expression on his face. It was clearly no more use as a weapon, so Bob hurled it at the Knight as hard as he could. The sword-stump struck the White Knight directly on the icon in the centre of his chest, making him flash with static and stagger back. Bob realized that that was the way to defeat the White Knight.

'The icon!' shouted Bob. 'Hit his icon!'

Immediately Dot launched a series of blows at the White Knight's icon. Each time she struck it, the Knight reeled back, flashing with static. However, the effort of the attack was exhausting Dot. Her blows became weaker and weaker until finally she fell to her knees.

The White Knight, although weakened himself, was still very dangerous. He moved towards Dot, raising his mace for one final blow. Bob saw the danger and launched himself across the room, knocking Dot out of the way. They landed in a heap.

Now they were both at the mercy of the White Knight. Enzo watched, helpless, as the Knight moved towards them. He had to do something. He drew back his arm and threw the megaphone at the knight with all his strength. It struck the knight directly on his chest icon. There was a flash of static and the knight began to fade out completely as he was sucked backwards out of the window.

'No way!' cried Enzo, amazed and delighted that he had managed to defeat the White Knight with such an inferior weapon.

There was a fanfare of trumpets and the Game Voice boomed: 'GAME OVER'.

The medieval landscape faded. There was a flash of white light and Bob, Dot and Enzo found themselves standing in the Diner car park wearing their normal clothes. Dot ran over and hugged Enzo.

'All right, Enzo! Nice shot.'

'Good job,' said Bob, rubbing his little friend's head affectionately.

'You mean it?' cried Enzo, thrilled that his hero was pleased with him.

'Yeah,' said Bob, smiling. Then he turned to Dot. 'All right,' he said. 'I give up. How did you get back to normal?'

'I was trying to tell you . . .' she replied. 'Al and I are partners in his business.' Then she smiled, as if the answer was obvious. 'I just vid-windowed for a delivery.'

Bob felt like an idiot, but he smiled anyway.

'You and Al? So much for me being Mr Save-The-Day.'

Bob offered Dot a rather mangled box. 'Care for some, uh, slightly used food?' he smiled.

'No,' said Dot, pulling a face, 'but thanks for the thought.'

Suddenly there was a desperate cry from behind them.

'BOB!'

Dot and Bob swung round and saw Enzo

55

being held in the air by a very annoyed looking Megabyte. Hack and Slash stood nearby, thinking about all the nasty things they'd like to do to Bob for making them look stupid.

'It was quite difficult and time consuming to process that magnet, Bob,' said Megabyte. 'I think I'd like it returned.' He lifted Enzo higher. 'And the sooner the better.'

Bob shrugged. 'No need to be so dramatic, M.B.'

He raised his left wrist. 'Glitch, tongs,' he commanded.

There was a *click-click-whirr* as Glitch transformed into a set of tongs that reached down on a telescopic arm and plucked the deadly magnet from its shielded case on Bob's belt. Bob smiled mischievously.

'I was just going to toss it anyway ... Here, catch!' he cried as Glitch whipped forward, hurling the magnet at Megabyte.

It was a perfect shot. The magnet struck Megabyte in the centre of his forehead with a clunk. He staggered back with the impact, sparking with static as he began to fade away, just as Dot had done earlier. Megabyte dropped Enzo as he desperately tried to remove the magnet, but he staggered back too far and toppled over the edge of a deep chasm that went right down to the very lowest levels of Mainframe. He shouted, 'Hack! Slash!' as he fell.

The two heavily armoured machines looked at each other. They knew there was very little they could do to help, but where their boss went, they would follow.

'Coming . . . Boss,' they declared between them as they jumped over the edge after Megabyte, chatting to each other about this and that. Finally there were three distant crashes followed by silence. Bob, Dot and Enzo looked over the edge.

'They're not even close to Al's,' said Bob, knowing that Megabyte would need a good deal of slow food to reverse the effect of the magnet.

'Nope,' agreed Dot.

They turned and headed back towards the

Diner. Bob went over the events of the day in his mind.

'While we're on the subject, Dot . . . is there anything in Mainframe you *don't* own?'

Dot smiled a knowing smile.

'Maybe,' she grinned. 'Who wants to know?'

Bob smiled and put his arms round his two friends as they headed back towards Dot's Diner for a well-earned rest.

Medusa Bug

Medusa Bug

Mainframe was always a very busy place. Everyone there had a function, and the sprites and binomes spent all their time responding to the constant flow of data and commands that streamed into the city from every direction. This took a lot of organisation, and much of that organisation was done by Dot Matrix. If she didn't know about something that was going on, it probably wasn't going on. Dot certainly worked very hard. Maybe, some of her friends thought, a little too hard.

In fact her little brother Enzo and Bob the guardian had decided to do something about it. They had turned up at Dot's Diner to carry out their plan. A little crowd of onlookers had gathered there. After all, this wasn't something you saw every day. Enzo was pulling Dot out of the Diner by her hand. Dot looked very worried but Enzo was waving cheerfully to the crowd.

'Bye, everyone! Don't wait for us!' he said with a big grin, but Dot suddenly broke away and turned back to the Diner.

'Oops. Just one more call, Enzo.' she pleaded.

This obviously wasn't going to be easy. Enzo grabbed Dot with both hands and stopped her.

'Dot! You need a break, and Bob's in a wait state outside. COME ON!!'

They headed for the door again, but just before they made it Dot turned back, muttering to herself. 'No really. I'm worried about the Mitchell account inputs. It'll just take a nanosecond.'

Enzo was disappointed.

'Dot?! You promised ... Remember that speech you gave me about keeping your promises? Dot? Hello?'

Dot came striding back. She was reluctant but she knew that a promise was a promise. She couldn't argue with that.

'I'm coming,' she said, and they left the Diner together. To be honest, she was curious as to where her little brother wanted to take her. He was being very mysterious. Suddenly Dot stopped in her tracks and stood staring at the sight that greeted her.

'Pretty cool, huh?' said Enzo with a smile.

There in front of them was Bob, the coolest sprite in Mainframe, sitting at the wheel of his vintage convertible air car which was hovering just off the ground. It was bright red with long, pointed wings on the back and lots of chrome *everywhere*. Although the engine was running, it sounded like it would rather be doing some- thing else – something like not running. She noticed the picnic basket on the back seat and saw that Bob was grinning like a proud parent. Dot was stunned.

'I don't believe it,' she said, staring open

mouthed. 'Bob? is your car actually . . . running?'

Bob gave a cocky smile.

'Yep!' he grinned. He was very proud of his old air car. Suddenly though, the car began to jerk and splutter like a faulty disc-drive. Bob frowned and gave the dashboard a good whack. The car lurched and began running normally again. Normally for an ancient, temperamental hovercar, that is. Bob smiled again.

'Isn't it awesome?' said Enzo, looking round at Dot, but she was gone. Enzo sighed. 'Oh not again!' he muttered to himself and headed back to the Diner. 'Dot!' he shouted. Bob joined Enzo at the door and they both stood there scowling as they watched Dot tapping away at data vid-windows while she talked to a secretary binome.

'. . . and the net codes? Formatted and docked?' asked Dot.

'Of course, Ms Matrix,' said the secretary binome.

'Please, call me Dot,' insisted Dot.

'Yes, Ms Matrix,' replied the secretary binome with unfailing politeness.

Bob and Enzo looked at each other. It was obvious that they wouldn't be able to get Dot away from the Diner by reasoning with her. However, there were always other options available to those with a little imagination and a certain amount of energy.

'Whaddya think, Enzo?' sighed Bob.

A look of determination crossed Enzo's face as he replied, 'Yeah, let's.'

Bob and Enzo strode across the Diner, looking like they meant business. There was a brief commotion, a flurry of arms and legs, and Bob and Enzo emerged from the diner, carrying Dot between them.

'Wait!' Dot laughed. 'Just one more call! That's all ... You two put me down.'

Bob and Enzo weren't listening though. They carried the protesting Dot over to the car and dumped her on to the back seat like a sack of data. She landed with an 'Oomph', and before she could leap out the automatic seatbelts had fastened and they shot off, quick as a flash, and headed for the lush green hills on the outskirts of the city. It looked like it was going to be a good day.

But things aren't always what they seem. At that very moment, in the City of Lost Angles, there was some serious trouble brewing.

GO TO

Imagine the Gilded Gate Bridge. Follow its twisted, shifting path across a sea of chaos to the dreadful floating Island where the City of Lost Angles stands. There, at the base of the bridge, two high-ranking Viral Binome Lieutenants wait anxiously for the return of their master. Their names are Hack and Slash, although neither one really knows which is which. This leads to a certain amount of confusion when orders are being given.

Hack and Slash didn't like being around that area because the City of Lost Angles was home to the dreadful Hexadecimal, Witch-Queen of Chaos and Malfunction, and there was always the possibility that she might turn up and do something seriously unpleasant to them. It took a lot to make Hack and Slash nervous. This was one of the reasons their master, Megabyte, had chosen them. In fact, apart from Megabyte himself, Hexadecimal was one of the few inhabitants of Mainframe that they would prefer *not* to tangle with. Of course there was always Bob as well, but they preferred not to dwell on the numerous times that Bob had made them look stupid.

Suddenly a sleek, black battle-wagon came swooping over the bridge, coming to a halt next to Hack and Slash. A panel slid aside with a mechanical whir and they saw Megabyte sitting inside. And he had something on his face that they hadn't seen before. It was a smile. He was holding something small in his hand.

At this point most inhabitants of Mainframe would have logged out of there or erased themselves with fright but the lieutenants were visibly relieved. They snapped to attention, eager for any news that would take them away from the dreaded bridge.

'Sir! What's our status?' asked one of them.

Megabyte smiled again, like a steel trap under pressure.

'After all the time, all the effort . . . all the lies. We finally have it.' And so saying he opened his hand to reveal a little angular box.

'Gentlemen,' he rumbled, in a voice that was designed for bad news, 'meet the Medusa.'

The lieutenants craned their necks to see the box. If they thought it didn't look like much they kept it to themselves, and gasped in awe.

'Finally,' said Hack – or it might have been Slash – 'Hexadecimal's ultimate weapon . . . a box!'

Megabyte gloated calmly, in the manner of one who knows that he's a powerful computer virus surrounded by idiots. The only thing Megabyte liked better than feeling superior was . . . well, nothing really. He felt a speech coming on.

'She thought she could hide its secret from me.' He said, getting into the swing of it, 'She thought she could develop a weapon this powerful without my knowledge.' He sighed with mock disappointment. 'Poor fool.'

Suddenly there was a massive explosion, the ground shook and chunks of debris fell all around as Hexadecimal erupted out of the ground wearing an EXTREMELY ANGRY mask. She looked like she was in the mood for pulling things apart, no matter how much those 'things' might object.

Megabyte, however, didn't even bother to look round to see what all the noise was about, which, given the circumstances, was a pretty cool thing to do. He just sat there, perfectly relaxed, and said, 'Oh, that would be her now.'

Hexadecimal came sweeping across the bridge towards them, hovering just above the ground, screaming 'MEGABYTE!!' like an overloaded soundblaster. A stream of nulls followed in her wake, like a river of data-rats. It was easy to form the impression that she was upset.

She confronted Megabyte, wearing her UTTERLY ENRAGED mask. 'You lied! you lied!' she spat. 'I was a fool to trust you.'

Megabyte just sat there, admiring his reflection in his claws. 'How true . . .' he replied, not in the least bit worried.

Hexadecimal paused and swiped on a THOUGHTFUL mask. 'It was, however, very clever the way you tricked me out of one of my toys.' Then she swiped on a CONFUSED mask. 'But what could you ever do with it?' she said in a puzzled tone. 'It's just a little trinket . . . You might as well give it back.'

She extended a hand with claws like needles, only sharper.

Megabyte just yawned and announced in a bored voice: 'Really, Hexadecimal, I don't have time for this.' He turned away, preparing to leave.

Hexadecimal put on her PITIFUL mask and said with mock sadness, 'Oh, how very, very sad!' and she sniffed, announcing, 'I'll have to destroy you all then.'

So saying, she motioned delicately with her great claws and the horde of nulls came rushing across the bridge in a screeching red and black tide.

Megabyte summoned Hack and Slash forwards with a casual gesture of his own. 'Well,' he declared, 'get to work, you two. I don't keep you around for your brains now, do I?'

Hack and Slash rolled forward, managing to say, 'No ... Sir ... Not our brains ... Absolutely not' between them. The mighty mechanicals positioned themselves in the centre of the bridge, facing the oncoming horde. Things weren't looking too good for them.

'This is it ... It's over now,' they thought, but then they had a brainwave. Bending down, they dug their metal fingers into the surface of the road. They muttered to themselves as they tried to get a grip: 'Oh, this is

heavy . . . This is not in my job description.'
Using their great strength, they managed to
tear loose the entire centre section of the
bridge and sent it crashing into the sea
below.

The foremost nulls were unable to stop in
time and plummeted into the dark chaos
below, leaving the rest to chomp and slobber
at the broken edge.

This failed to improve Hexadecimal's
temper. Sliding on an EXTREMELY MAD
mask, she screamed, 'THEN I SHALL
SMITE YOU MYSELF, DOG!' She laughed
in the manner of an evil genius and flew
towards Megabyte, enveloped in a cloud of
angry static.

Megabyte seemed unimpressed. He
turned to his communications unit and gave
a casual order to his troops. 'Gentlemen,
show the lady some of our own toys, won't
you? I'll see you back at the Tor.' Then he
glided off smugly.

The lieutenant in charge of Megabyte's
forces made a complicated gesture with his

hand (that he had been practising in front of
the mirror to make it look as dramatic as
possible) and a legion of ABC armoured
vehicles thundered dramatically into view
over the ridge opposite the bridge, hovering
in tight formation. Hatches whirred open
and an impressive array of rockets, cannons
and lasers slid into view.

The commander gave his favourite hand
gesture again and every vehicle opened fire
unleashing a devastating barrage at Hexadecimal that would have blown the socks off
a lesser sprite. However, with a wave of her
clawed hand, Hexadecimal created an invisible force field around herself. The entire
barrage exploded harmlessly against the
force-field, leaving her completely un-
harmed.

Eventually the armoured vehicles ran out
of ammunition. Hexadecimal dropped her
force-field and smiled the sort of smile that
implied she wasn't about to invite you to
tea. The lieutenant in charge of the army
didn't have a hand gesture rehearsed for

this occasion. He could think of a few leg gestures and they all involved running, but he knew he wouldn't get very far. Then Hexadecimal slid a VERY ANGRY INDEED mask into place and pointed her closed fist towards the legion of ABCs and, well, you really don't want to know what happened next. Suffice to say it made a dreadful mess.

Meanwhile Megabyte, closely followed by his mechanical minions, Hack and Slash, was racing away from the island battle. He might be a power-hungry monster but he wasn't stupid.

GO TO

Imagine the silicon Tor rising above Mainframe in the shape of a colossal cobra. This is Megabyte's laboratory. A vid-window is open and Megabyte is talking to one of his lieutenants who looks dazed and defeated. The remains of his legion of ABCs lie battered and sparking in the background. The lieutenant is trying to describe what happened.

'. . . then, out of nowhere, she said something about being bored, and just . . . disappeared.' The lieutenant saluted with as much dignity as he could manage in his battered state. 'Perimeter secured, sir,' he said, trying to sound as if he had won a great victory, just like commanders of soldiers have always done. Megabyte closed the vid-window.

'Very well,' he said to himself and turned his attention to the box containing the Medusa that rested in his claw. He turned it around, admiring it. Megabyte approached Hack and Slash and said in his most innocent voice, 'It was all her fault, you know. Her increased security and strict privacy led me to my victory. She was so careful. So secretive.' Then he smiled evilly. 'I knew she was up to something.'

Megabyte held the box near a vid-window in order to scan the contents. The display showed statistics and line graphs, x-ray images and text, but Megabyte still looked puzzled and tapped away at the controls of the vid-window, muttering to himself, 'And yet, despite the length and scope of our operation, we still do not know the true nature of the Medusa's power . . . Until now.'

Megabyte smiled triumphantly and touched a section of the box. The centre section rose up and rotated in a very businesslike manner. Then the six facets on top of the box opened like a digital flower. It certainly looked as if it was about to do something very impressive.

In fact, it was just about to do something very impressive, but not exactly the sort of impressive thing Megabyte might have hoped for. A look of horror crossed his face as the claw holding the box began to turn to stone, the marble-like texture spreading up his arm with an evil, crackling sound.

'No!' he bellowed, and dropped the box. From where it landed, the stone spread across the floor in every direction. Megabyte grasped his arm in horror. 'No! This is no weapon! It is a viral bug!'

The minions in the room were in a panic

as they tried to escape but one by one they were transformed into petrified statues. Hack and Slash looked down at their bodies as the virus spread upwards and managed an 'Uh . . . Oh' between them before they too became frozen, falling over with a mighty thud – two more victims of the Medusa virus.

Megabyte, meanwhile, was tapping away furiously at a vid-window with his unin-fected hand in a desperate attempt to halt the virus. 'Computer: identify virus. Full scan. List possible cures and counteracting agents.' He leaned close to the screen, des-perate to find a cure, but the calm computer voice informed him, 'File type: unknown. Counter agents: unknown. Cure options: un-known.'

Suddenly there was a burst of static and the staring face of Hexadecimal appeared in the vid-window. Megabyte recoiled in hor-ror. Hexadecimal spoke in a mock computer voice to taunt Megabyte: 'Getting your sorry self out of trouble: unknown.' Then she laughed like a little schoolgirl, delighted at how clever she had been. 'I see you found my little surprise! Hee hee! Isn't it sweet?' she said with glee, covering her mouth with her hand as she tried not to laugh.

Megabyte was furious. 'You! All this time! All your secrecy! All your security! My whole operation, a trap!'

Hexadecimal could hardly contain her delight. 'Yes, yes,' she announced joyfully, but suddenly changed her expression into an ARROGANT mask. 'Now I suppose you'll want thanks for all your hard work.'

Megabyte screamed in rage but there was nothing he could do. The deadly virus continued to spread across his body until, finally, he was turned completely to stone. He fell forward, the red glow of his eyes shone briefly, but then they too were extinguished.

And yet the virus continued to spread. Down the sides of the Tor it went, and out on to the surrounding land. It wouldn't have taken a genius to work out that Mainframe was in serious trouble.

GO TO

In the middle of the City of Lost Angles there is a massive circular theatre-type building with a raised stage in the centre. In the middle of the stage is a throne and it was here that Hexadecimal liked to sit, in company with her sly little pet, Scuzzy to accompany her.

She watched the spread of the Medusa via a vid-window. 'I hope this was the right thing to do. Infect the whole world with an unstoppable bug? Um, I'm not sure.' But suddenly she threw back her head, swiped on a LAUGHTER mask and her mad cackles echoed through the halls of her retreat as a spotlight hovered in the air before her, illuminating her as she sat, laughing insanely. She was the star in her own one-woman show.

GO TO

Imagine a small park on the edge of town.

Cars and utility vehicles rush past on their way into and out of the city. However, one of the hover cars doesn't seem to be going anywhere. In fact it's not even hovering. Dot is lying on a blanket on the grass, surrounded by picnic things. It might not be the ideal place for a picnic, but she is making the best of it. Bob has his head under the bonnet of his old car. Enzo looks on hopefully.

Dot sat up and called over: 'Nice picnic, guys.'

Bob leaned out from under the bonnet, holding a spanner. He scowled at the comment. 'I'm working here, okay, I'm working!' he declared.

'You want some help?' asked Dot sweetly.

Bob just glared and ducked back under the bonnet. Dot shrugged and looked around. Maybe they hadn't made it to the ideal picnic spot, but at least it was somewhere she could relax, away from the pressures of the Diner, even if they had only managed to get a little way before the car broke down. She took a deep breath.

'Don't get me wrong,' she said. 'I gotta admit, it is kind of nice to get away from it all.'

Bob popped out from under the car said 'You're welcome,' and slid back under the vehicle.

Dot chuckled, 'Thank you.'

Suddenly Enzo heard barking that sounded strangely familiar. He stepped away from the car and stared into the distance where the barking seemed to be coming from. He was right. It was indeed his canine pal, Frisket, but something was wrong. In the distance Frisket was galloping towards them. He was being pursued by the Medusa bug which was speeding across the ground with an evil crackling sound.

'Check it out,' said Enzo in horror. 'Something weird is chasing Frisket.'

Bob stopped hammering away at the engine and came to look. The dog was just managing to stay ahead of the spreading stone-texture but another strand had crossed in front of him, cutting him off. The virus formed a circle around him and began to close in. Frisket growled menacingly. The group at the car looked on with concern.

'Frisket?' muttered Enzo. He was clearly worried.

Suddenly there was a howling yelp that cut off as abruptly as it had started.

Enzo screamed, 'FRISKET!' and lunged forward, but Dot grabbed him and held on. Frisket, now completely made of stone, toppled sideways and hit the ground with a loud thud. Enzo was going crazy, trying to climb out of the car, but Dot managed to hold on to him as he shouted, 'Frisket! Let me go! DOT! We gotta help him!'

Dot tried to calm him, saying, 'Enzo! Enzo! Wait! We don't know what that thing is yet.'

They both looked across at Bob for an answer. Bob had converted his wrist unit, Glitch, into a stat-scanner that he was now studying intently. 'Unknown file type. This is bad. Very bad,' he stated grimly.

Dot pointed down the road. 'Uh, Bob? I think we're next,' she said nervously as Enzo jumped back into the car.

Bob held up the scanner and had to agree. 'I think you're right. Glitch? Ignition.' Glitch changed into a joystick with a key-shaped stem. Bob tossed Glitch to Dot and dived back under the car. 'Quick!' he shouted. 'Try her again.'

Dot inserted Glitch into the keyhole on the dashboard and turned. There was a growling sound from the engine but it wouldn't start. The Medusa bug raced towards them like a stone wave.

'Again!' shouted Bob. Again the car would not start.

Dot watched in horrified fascination. 'Uh, Boys?' she said nervously.

The Medusa bug approached rapidly as the car tried to turn over: 'RRRrrrRRR, RRRrrrRRR.'

Suddenly Enzo stood up in the front seat and whacked the dashboard, just as Bob had done earlier outside the Diner. The bug was

85

about to engulf the car when the engine coughed into life. Dot put her foot down and the car shot forward, giving Bob just enough time to leap into the back seat where he landed in a rather un-heroic heap. One thing you can say about Bob's car though. When it does go, it goes VERY fast.

Enzo looked back forlornly. 'But Frisket!' he said sadly as they sped away from the terrible scene.

Dot turned and tried to comfort him. 'Enzo, we can't help Frisket if the same thing happens to us. Don't worry, we'll be back . . . when we know what we're dealing with.' She looked worriedly at Bob. 'Bob, what is that thing?'

Bob just stared straight ahead.

'We need to see Phong,' he said grimly. 'Now.'

GO TO

Imagine a huge, spherical building that floats in mid air. It is attached to the land by

*five slender bridges. This is the principle
office of Mainframe. Bob, Dot and Enzo are
in Phong's anteroom. They are all studying a
vid-window map showing the infected areas
of the city in red. It is spreading everywhere
and heading for the centre where the Principle Office itself stands.*

Phong spoke seriously.

'It is a bug. Pure and simple. It can and
will spread to anything it touches. We are
all at risk.' Phong turned from the screen.
'You, Bob, may be immune since you are a
Guardian. It is difficult to tell.'

'Trust me,' Bob replied. 'I don't want to
find out.' He began pacing back and forth.
'But I do want to get out there and warn
everybody,' he said with feeling.

Dot stopped him with a gentle hand.

'We need a plan first,' she said. She was
right.

Enzo glared angrily at the screen. 'Poor
old Frisket. I bet ol' Megadump is behind all

this.' He turned to the others. 'I say we crash his tower. Big time.'

Phong tapped away at the vid-window controls, Dot looked thoughtful. Bob continued pacing as he said, 'I don't know, Enzo, this one isn't his style. It's too unpredictable. Too dangerous.'

Phong studied the stats on the screen. 'It's completely random. Almost chaotic.'

Dot and Bob looked at each other in sudden realization.

'Hexadecimal?' said Dot.

'Bingo!' declared Bob.

As he said this, Phong pulled up multiple live images of Mainframe on his vid-window. They could see Megabyte's Silicon Tor standing like a frozen statue like most of the rest of the city. All except the City of Lost Angles. The Medusa bug had not crossed the Gilded Gate Bridge.

'It must be her,' declared Phong. 'Look, even the Tor has been infected.'

'But not Hex's island,' remarked Enzo.

'Hexadecimal, eh?' sighed Bob, turning to

his wise old friend. 'This one's got me worried, Phong. I mean, that Hex is as loopy as
they come.'

Phong nodded seriously. Enzo looked up
at Dot. 'Bob worried?' he said with awe.
'Dude.'

Phong was checking more data on the
screen.

'Worse still, children, is the fact that the
longer something (or someone) is infected,
the greater the chance of decay. See here – '
and he indicated a road sign at the edge of
the city that was beginning to crumble. 'Low
energy goes first,' he explained, 'like this
sign. But then high energy goes next.'

A grim expression crossed Dot's face.
'High energy . . . Sprites like us.'

'And Frisket!' yelled Enzo. Phong nodded.
'That's not even funny!' declared Enzo.
'What are we gonna do?'

Phong took charge. 'Dot,' he said. 'You
and Enzo get everyone evacuated from the
city. It is next in the bug's path.'

'Right,' said Dot.

Then Phong turned to Bob.

'Bob, you come with me. We must hurry.'

Phong then turned to the wall and said the password, 'Greek action'. A secret doorway opened and Phong disappeared inside. Bob began to follow but could not help looking back over his shoulder with the awful thought that he might never see his two friends again.

He shouted back, 'Hey, you two be careful out there!'

Dot and Enzo trotted towards the anteroom exit. Dot looked back with a sad face. 'You too,' she said.

Then Bob disappeared down the secret corridor to join Phong in the infinite space of the Archives. Floating windows shot past on zip-boards. All the knowledge of Mainframe was stored here but Bob knew exactly what he was looking for.

'I'll need two high-lined viricidals, self adjusting, and a level eight desktop rebuilder, wide fielding.'

Phong stopped dead in his tracks and turned around, shaking his head.

'This is not the Super Computer, Bob.' He gestured towards a nearby window. 'I'm afraid this is all we have to offer.'

Bob moved closer to look at the little pink object that Phong held in his hand. It looked like the sort of rubber eraser that young sprites might use in school.

'Virus Erase Command?' he said, looking at Phong with concern. 'Don't you think that's a little primitive?'

Phong sighed. 'Perhaps, but it is the best we have.'

Bob stood in thought with his hand on his chin.

'Hmmm . . . I suppose if we boost its power with an add-on it might do the trick. Crude, but simple.'

Phong gave him the small Virus Erase Command unit.

'Then let us make it so.'

GO TO

A long line of Mainframe citizens was filing

91

down the thin bridges of the Principle Office. They were slumped and sad looking. One large binome was carrying Cecil, the waiter from Dot's Diner. He was not a happy waiter.

'Sacre Bleu!' he declared, waggling his moustache with irritation. 'I am a dedicated server, not a piece of luggage!'

One binome was carrying a baby binome in her arms. The baby was carrying a small teddy bear. They both looked very frightened.

Dot and Enzo stood either side of the long line of sprites and binomes that were flooding into the principle office. More and more transporters of every kind were arriving, bringing anxious citizens who were hoping to find safety in the massive building.

'Chin up,' said Dot, trying to be cheerful, 'we're almost there.'

Suddenly a binome stopped and pointed skyward.

'Bob! It's Bob!' he yelled, hopefully. Everyone on the bridge looked up and saw Bob emerge from a opening in the office, flying on a zip-board. He was carrying the Virus Eraser. It was fixed to a complicated-looking device, which was the add-on power booster. The crowd cheered as Bob waved and shot off across the city to do battle with the Medusa bug.

Enzo was excited. 'All right, Bob! Woo hoo! You show them they can't mess with us! Crunch its format! Kick that bug's bit map. For Frisket!'

Dot stood quietly nearby, watching as Bob sped off.

'Be careful, Bob,' she said softly to herself.

GO TO

Imagine Mainframe as an abandoned city. Air cars, taxis and go-subs litter the streets. All is quiet apart from an eerie cracking sound that seems to be approaching. All of a sudden the Medusa bug sweeps across the scene, engulfing all in its path, leaving a cold, quiet world of stone in its wake. It spreads up buildings and down pillars to attack the lower levels. Nowhere is safe. Even the elegant energy fountain is petrified in mid-flow.

Watching all this, from the safety of her lair, was Hexadecimal, so excited by all the chaos she had caused that she couldn't decide which mask to wear. On a vid-window shaped like a gold-framed magic mirror she was watching re-runs of the moment that Megabyte's Tor was overrun by the Medusa bug.

'Wow! Ohh! Did you see that, Scuzzy?' she asked her pet. Then, wearing a SAD mask, she said, 'How sad. All of Mainframe. Doomed.' Then she laughed like a maniac. No-one could accuse her of being a well-balanced individual. The normally sly and devious Scuzzy shivered with fear in a dark corner. Suddenly Hexadecimal slid on a SURPRISED mask and stared at her vid-window, which showed Bob gliding on to the scene.

'What's this? Bob the Guardian? Oh no, Oh no!' But then she relaxed, putting on a FASCINATED mask: 'Oh, yes . . .' she said. 'Won't this be interesting?'

Unaware that he was being watched, Bob cautiously approached the spreading bug and pulled the pin from the anti-virus command unit. He activated the unit. It began to beep rapidly.

'All right, you antique,' he said, aiming it carefully, 'do your thing.' He hurled it to the ground and zipped off as fast as his zip-board would carry him.

The anti-virus command fell towards the petrified ground below then, just before it hit, it exploded in a blinding ball of energy. Bob was almost knocked from his zip-board by the blast. He looked round to see the explosive energy spreading across the infected areas of Mainframe. It was turning everything back to normal!

Back in the City of Lost Angles, Hexadecimal slipped on a WORRIED mask and gasped. 'My poor Medusa!'

Back at the Principle Office all the residents cheered happily. Across the city, Bob looked down on the scene and smiled. However, his smile soon faded. As he watched, the cleansing ripples running across the Medusa began to slow. The Medusa was resisting the anti-virus and energy sparks flared here and there until suddenly the ripples faltered and broke up. The virus was spreading again, as fast as ever.

'This is not good,' Bob said to himself as the Medusa began spreading towards him. 'Where's a game cube when you need one?' he wondered.

Back at the Principle Office the crowd panicked again and began to rush inside. There was only one happy person in the whole of Mainframe. In her lair, Hexadecimal was wearing her ELATED mask and doing a jolly little jig around the room, singing: 'Happy, happy, happy!'

Phong was not so happy as he hurried the last of the citizens to safety. He pushed some buttons that had appeared before him in the shiny wall, and the long bridges of the Principle Office began to draw inward into the body of the huge spherical building and armoured shutters closed over four of the five doors. Phong, Dot and Enzo were left watching anxiously outside the fifth door for their friend.

'Come on, Bob. You can make it,' said Enzo softly as Bob appeared in the distance, speeding towards them with the Medusa hot on his trail.

Bob arrived at the Principle Office and stood before Dot and Enzo looking defeated. He had tried, but it hadn't been good enough. They rushed inside. Phong closed the last door and retracted the bridges that linked the building to the rest of the city. Shields descended to cover the doors. Then he activated a powerful force-field around the building. The room vibrated with energy. Inside, the citizens of Mainframe sat around in little groups, waiting to see what their fate would be. Outside, the blue-white force-field surrounded the globe of the Principle Office as it floated in the air, and yet already the Medusa was sending out crystal-like extensions to bridge the gap.

Inside the office the Mainframers watched the monitors with concern. At first, pieces of the bug were burnt off as they touched the powerful force-field, but soon it began to spread into the defending energy itself, gradually replacing the glow of the force-field with the crackling stone-texture of the Medusa. The field was completely transformed. Then the covering of stone started crumbling on to the top of the Principle Office and the Medusa began to spread along its very surface.

There was panic as the helpless citizens within were rapidly turned to stone by the bug as it worked its way from the corners of the room.

The Medusa spread up the binome carrying Cecil the waiter who complained bitterly in his French accent. 'This day! She is miserables! First I am detached from mah ceiling ... and now Thees!' But he said no more, as he too was turned to stone.

The little baby binome was hugged by its mother as it cried. It dropped its teddy bear and the little toy was instantly turned to stone, just like everything else.

Across the room Bob was trying in vain to reach his friends. 'Dot! Enzo!' he shouted over the panicking crowd, but they couldn't hear. They were cornered by the approaching bug in another part of the room. Dot pulled Enzo close and they both squinted their eyes as the bug struck. Enzo managed to shout, 'DOT!' before they were both turned completely to stone.

Meanwhile Phong was tapping away at a vid-window, trying to find an answer to the deadly bug. He didn't even stop when the bug began eating up his body. He just kept on tapping until he too had been completely turned to stone.

Bob was the last citizen of Mainframe left. He was backed into a corner as the bug advanced. He used Glitch as a laser gun to try and halt the Medusa.

'No! No! I won't let you!' he shouted, but it

was no good. The bug began to spread up his body, leaving him frozen in stone.

Now the office was silent. All the citizens of Mainframe were petrified, like statues in a museum. Hexadecimal had won.

But wait. There was a tiny sound, a slight motion in the corner. Then a cracking CRASH as Bob exploded from the thin covering of stone that had formed around him. As a Guardian he was immune to the virus. But what could he do? He looked around the room in disbelief.

'NO!! . . .' He screamed, but the sound just echoed around the room until all was silent again. He slid to the floor, cradling his head in his hands. Defeated.

Eventually he rose and began to walk through the forest of statues. He stopped at wise old Phong.

'You were right, old friend. I am immune.' And looking round he added sadly, 'lucky me.' He walked over to where Dot and Enzo stood, and as he looked at them his face grew firm with determination.

'Let Hexadecimal turn all my friends into stone? Destroy Mainframe? And get away with it?' A mischievous smile crossed his face. 'I DON'T THINK SO.'

GO TO

Hexadecimal sat on her throne, in the centre of her vast theatre. Around the stage floated frozen statues of sprites and binomes – all that remained of the citizens of Mainframe.

'How do you like my new garden, Scuzzy?' she asked her nasty little pet. 'It holds up so much better than some of my earlier efforts.'

As she spoke, however, one of the binomes crumbled to dust. 'Well, for now at least . . .' she remarked. 'Does it please you, Scuzzy?' she inquired.

But Scuzzy didn't respond. He just floated before his mistress, silently, for he too had been turned to stone by the Medusa.

Hexadecimal put on an ANGRY mask and shouted, 'I asked you a question!' but of course there was still no reply. She waved her arm and Scuzzy drifted away. Hexadecimal sat there, silently. A shadow shifted in the background.

Bob appeared behind her, high up, at the back of the huge hall. He shot out a Glitch-line and slid down it. He zoomed across the stage and struck Hexadecimal from behind, trying to knock her into the hovering form of Scuzzy so that she too would be infected by the Medusa, but Hexadecimal stopped short, hanging in mid-air.

'Funny,' she said. 'I sense a presence.'

'That would be ME!' replied Bob as he landed on the stage, facing Hexadecimal.

'That's a good one, Guardian,' she declared. 'Infect me with the Medusa. How delightfully clever.'

'Why, thank you,' said Bob. He watched her warily as she narrowed her eyes, hiding her right hand behind her back while she built up a ball of energy there. Bob too reached behind his back. There, attached to his belt, was the little stone figure of the baby binome's teddy bear, infected with the virus.

Bob grabbed the bear like a gun-fighter and hurled it at Hexadecimal. She was momentarily surprised, but quickly raised a finger and the bear stopped in mid-air just in front of her face. Her expression changed to a DISAPPOINTED mask.

'Now we can't have any of that, young man.' She shook her head slowly. 'And you? Immune to my Medusa. Tsk, tsk, tsk. How very disappointing. I'll just have to destroy you the old-fashioned way,' she growled, wearing an EVIL SMILING mask.

She launched herself into the air and hurtled towards Bob with a blood-curdling scream. Bob tried to reel himself out of the way on his Glitch line before Hexadecimal caught him. He shot upwards, but Hexadecimal made a hand gesture and Bob stopped dead in mid-air, hanging there, completely at the mercy of the Queen of Chaos.

'Not so fast, Bob,' said Hexadecimal, sliding on an EVIL mask. 'As much as I enjoy the chaos you bring into my life . . . it is time to be rid of you once and for all.' And with that she pulled back her hand for the final blow, her curled claw glowing and sparking with energy.

Bob decided that this might be a good time to think fast.

'Uh, I like how you've changed Mainframe,' he said, pleasantly.

Hexadecimal now wore an INTERESTED mask.

'Do you?' she asked. 'And why is that, my love?'

Bob smiled.

'Well, now that everything is set in stone, you've made Mainframe so predictable.'

Hexadecimal put on a PUZZLED mask. 'What do you mean?' she inquired.

Bob was still dangling in mid-air, locked in her invisible grip.

'Well,' he said, 'everyone in the same spot. Never changing. Never moving. Nothing but still and quiet.' Bob smiled a charming smile. 'How very peaceful it will all be now,' he remarked.

Hexadecimal put on a WORRIED mask.

'Peaceful? Oh, dear. How true.'

She began to step back, deep in thought. Her invisible grip on Bob began to weaken and he was lowered gently to the ground. He continued to speak.

'No more battles with Megabyte . . .'

Hexadecimal covered her ears in panic.

'Quiet!' she shouted. 'Silence!'

Bob stepped forward.

'No more unexpected turn of events,' he pointed out. For the Queen of Chaos this was just too awful to contemplate. She backed away from him, putting on a PANIC mask.

'NO! NO! WHAT HAVE I DONE? NO!'

Bob carried on in a gentle voice: 'Just peace . . . and calm . . . forever . . .'

Hexadecimal finally cracked.

'NO! NOOO! I MUST STOP IT ALL FROM GOING SO VERY WRONG!'

Then suddenly she smiled, raised her hand casually, and clicked her fingers. A rushing wave spread across Mainframe like a silent explosion. Everywhere it went things were turned back to normal. It reached the Principle Office and with a WHOOSH all the citizens were cured of the Medusa bug and stood there, surprised, trying to remember what had happened. (Then when they did, they tried to forget.) Enzo and Dot returned to normal and smiled at each other. Dot gave her little brother a big hug. The energy sped onwards like a wave of change, returning the whole of Mainframe to normal.

Bob watched as Hexadecimal drifted off into the shadows of her strange theatre.

'Now that is one strange lady,' he said to himself. Even the restored Scuzzy seemed to agree.

Bob was eager to see if his friends were OK and headed back towards the Principle Office. He needn't have worried. They were all fine.

GO TO

Enzo chased an unusually playful Frisket across an open field as the sea shimmered in the background. Dot was lounging next to a picnic basket, looking totally relaxed, if not a little sleepy. This was most unlike Dot. In the background, Bob walked away from his car with a satisfied grin.

'It's one miracle after another. First I fix my car. Then I save the World from the brink of destruction.' He settled down next to Dot. 'But most incredibly, Enzo and I actually get you to relax.'

Dot smiled.

'You should both get a medal,' she said, relaxing even more.

'Thanks,' said Bob, 'but I think I'll settle for a long nap instead.'

Suddenly game alarms blared, shattering the silence. Their eyes opened wide as a game cube began descending from the sky and a voice boomed out: 'Warning: Incoming game. Warning: Incoming game.'

'Oh well,' thought Bob, 'just another day in Mainframe.'

The ReBoot Glossary

Enzo's Guide to Super Coolness

ALPHANUMERIC (pronounced alpha-new-merick): Great; wow; unbelievable.

ACCESS: Get; e.g. 'Can I access your attention?'

BASIC: Stupid; 'I must be basic, low res., downsided, erasable.' 'Has he gone low density or what?'

COOL: Often used in combination; e.g. 'Whoa, coolness'; 'super cooled'; 'no way! coolness'.

COMPILE UP: Cheer up, e.g. 'Compile up, act your age.'

DIPSWITCH: Egg brain; e.g. 'Okay, you dip-switch, prepare to meet your programmer!'

DOOMED: Done for; e.g. 'We're doomed, logged off, archived, quit without saving.' The opposite of 'In the prime of your input/ouput'.

FUNCTIONAL: All there; e.g. 'Is he fully functional?'

HIGH DENSITY: Important, major; e.g. 'We're talking high density here.'

NETWORK: as in 'What in the Network are you talking about?' Also, to 'get on'; eg 'Are we networking here?'

NULLIFIED: Terminated; e.g. 'What are you trying to do, get us nullified?'

PIXELACIOUS: (pronounced pix-el-ay-shus) Brilliant; fab; wonderful.

PROCESSED: On top of it; worked out; e.g. 'I've got it all processed.'

PROGRAM: Get with it; e.g. 'Get with the program or you're history.'

QUIT FILE: Give up; e.g. 'Don't quit file so easily.'

Honourable mentions in the cool quip department also go to:

'Find someone else's energy to eat – go and annoy someone else, you termite.'

'Man, you're really out of it.'

'I guess I'd better scare us up some transport!'

ZOOL

MEET ZOOL, THE ALIEN NINJA FROM THE NTH DIMENSION

'Cooler than Mario, smarter than Sonic . . . '

Two things Zool is not!
1. Boring . . .
2. An ant. This is a vile lie put about by his arch enemy Mental Block. Ants are small, hard working insects with lots of legs, Zool is an alien from outer space with breath-taking powers. Also ants do not have their names written on the soles of their shoes. And Zool does, so there!

ZOOL RULES
Isbn: 0 7522 0952 3

Coming soon:
COOL ZOOL
Isbn: 0 7522 0957 4

MIGHTY MORPHIN POWER RANGERS

The Mighty Morphin Power Rangers are teenagers with special abilities brought together to defend the Earth against an intergalactic sorceress named Rita. Drawing strength from the spirits of ancient dinosaurs, the Rangers also benefit from the futuristic technology given to them by the inter-dimensional being, Zordon.

IT'S MORPHIN TIME!
Isbn: 0 7522 0939 6

MEGAZORD TO THE RESCUE!
Isbn: 0 7522 0944 2

THE TERROR TOAD
Isbn: 0 7522 0949 3

RITA'S REVENGE
Isbn: 0 7522 0954 X

TAKE THAT

Introducing the books every
Take That fan should read!

TAKE THAT –
OUR STORY

Piers Morgan

The hottest band in Britain are talented, down-to-earth,
funny and hard working. Now, for the first time, the
boys have told their own amazing story.

Isbn: 1 85283 839 6

TAKE THAT ON THE ROAD
Piers Morgan

Take That have taken the charts by storm and driven teenage girls mad all over the world with their fresh-faced good looks and slick dance routines. This book takes a behind-the-scenes look at Take That on tour and gives an insight into this incredibly popular band.

Isbn: 1 85283 396 3

TAKE THAT UNDER MY PILLOW

This gift pack of five mini books in a slipcase is essential reading for any Take That fan. Each book is devoted to one of the stars of the band and contains twenty exclusive photographs with their fact files and quotes.

Isbn: 0 7522 0988 4

SAVED BY THE BELL

This hit US teen show follows the inventive schemes and mischievous dreams of Bayside High's wacky students. Now on Channel Four Television, Saved By The Bell looks set to become as popular in the UK as it has been in the States.

Novelisations:

ZACK'S LAST SCAM
Isbn: 0 7522 0990 6

ZACK STRIKES BACK
Isbn: 0 7522 0985 X

GIRLS' NIGHT OUT
Isbn: 0 7522 0901 9

ONE WILD WEEKEND
Isbn: 0 7522 0955 7

SUPER SAVED BY THE BELL SCRAPBOOK
Isbn: 0 7522 0961 2

CALIFORNIA DREAMS

The hit TV teen show, California Dreams, has been
described as a cross between *Beverly Hills 90210* and
The Monkees. Superhunk, Jake, and his high school
friends form a rock band called ... California Dreams.

Novelisations:

PLAYING FOR KEEPS
Isbn: 0 7522 0916 7

PERFECT HARMONY
Isbn: 0 7522 0906 X

WHO CAN YOU TRUST?
Isbn: 0 7522 0911 6

HOW TO ORDER YOUR BOXTREE BOOKS

HORROR HIGH

☐ 0 7522 0996 3	*Bad Moon Rising*	£2.99
☐ 0 7522 0971 X	*Rave On!*	£2.99
☐ 1 85283 358 0	*Symphony of Terror*	£2.99
☐ 1 85283 363 7	*Demon Brood*	£2.99

ZOOL

☐ 0 7522 0952 3	*Zool Rules*	£3.99
☐ 0 7522 0957 4	*Cool Zool*	£3.99

MIGHTY MORPHIN POWER RANGERS

☐ 0 7522 0939 6	*It's Morphin Time*	£2.99
☐ 0 7522 0944 2	*Megazord To The Rescue*	£2.99
☐ 0 7522 0949 3	*The Terror Toad*	£2.99
☐ 0 7522 0954 X	*Rita's Revenge*	£2.99
☐ 0 7522 0879 9	*The Bumble Beast*	£2.99
☐ 0 7522 0889 6	*Bad Dream Machine*	£2.99
☐ 0 7522 0894 2	*Super Zords!*	£2.99

TAKE THAT

☐ 1 85283 839 6	*Our Story*	£5.99
☐ 1 85283 396 3	*On The Road*	£5.99
☐ 0 7522 0988 4	*Under My Pillow*	£5.99

SAVED BY THE BELL

☐ 0 7522 0990 6	*Zack's Last Scam*	£3.50
☐ 0 7522 0985 X	*Zack Strikes Back*	£3.50
☐ 0 7522 0901 9	*Girls' Night Out*	£3.50
☐ 0 7522 0955 7	*One Wild Weekend*	£3.50
☐ 0 7522 0961 2	*Super Saved By The Bell Scrapbook*	£3.99

CALIFORNIA DREAMS

☐ 0 7522 0916 7	*Playing For Keeps*	£3.50
☐ 0 7522 0906 X	*Perfect Harmony*	£3.50
☐ 0 7522 0911 6	*Who Can You Trust?*	£3.50

All these books are available at your local bookshop or newsagent, or can be ordered direct from the publisher. Just tick the titles you want and fill in the form below.

Prices and availability subject to charge without notice.

Boxtree Cash Sales, P.O. Box 11, Falmouth, Cornwall TR10 9EN

Please send a cheque or postal order for the value of the book and add the following for postage and packing:

U.K. including B.F.P.O. – £1.00 for one book plus 50p for the second book, and 30p for each additional book ordered up to a £3.00 maximum.

Overseas including Eire – £2.00 for the first book plus £1.00 for the second book, and 50p for each additional book ordered.

OR please debit this amount from my Access/Visa Card (delete as appropriate).

Card Number ☐☐☐☐☐☐☐☐☐☐☐☐☐☐☐☐

Amount £ ....

Expiry Date on card ....

Signed ....

Name ....

Address ....